**Give your child a head start with
PICTURE READERS**

Dear Parent,

Now children as young as preschool age can have the fun and satisfaction of reading a book all on their own.

In every Picture Reader, there are simple words, rebus pictures, and 24 flash cards to cut out and keep. (There is a flash card for every rebus picture plus extra cards for reading practice.) After children listen to each story a couple of times, they will be ready to try it all by themselves.

Collect all the titles in our Picture Reader series. Once children have mastered these books, they can move on to Levels 1, 2, and 3 in our All Aboard Reading series.

For my dear father-in-law,
Dr. Edward F. Lewison, with warm wishes
for many happy, snowy days—W.C.L.

To the snow-loving children of the Clark and
Wilkins Elementary Schools, Amherst, N.H.
Warm wishes—M.C-L.

Text copyright © 2000 by Wendy Cheyette Lewison. Illustrations copyright © 2000 by Maryann Cocca-Leffler. All rights reserved. Published by Grosset & Dunlap, a division of Penguin Putnam Books for Young Readers, New York. GROSSET & DUNLAP and ALL ABOARD READING are trademarks of Penguin Putnam Inc. Published simultaneously in Canada. Printed in the U.S.A. Library of Congress Catalog Card Number: 00-131223

ISBN 0-448-42184-4   A B C D E F G H I J

ALL ABOARD READING™

A PICTURE READER

The
BIG
SNOWBALL

By Wendy Cheyette Lewison
Illustrated by Maryann Cocca-Leffler

Grosset & Dunlap • New York

Up on a

that was very tall,

a little

made a big .

He gave that 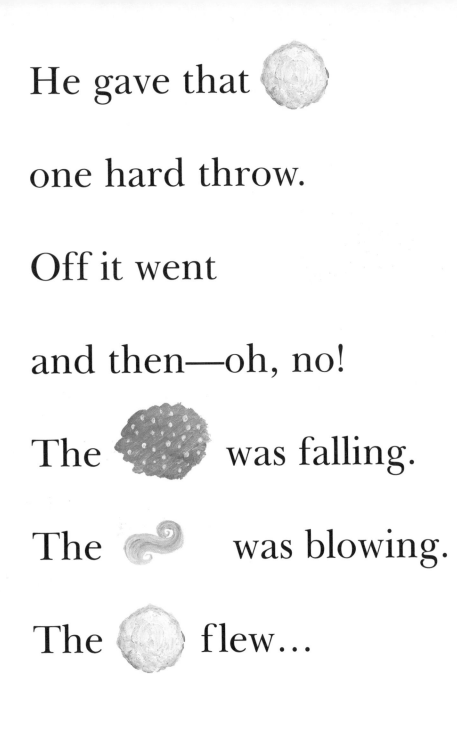 one hard throw.

Off it went

and then—oh, no!

The 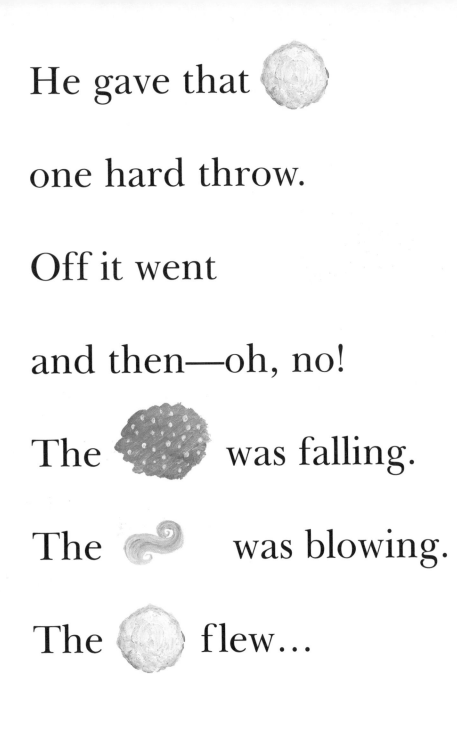 was falling.

The 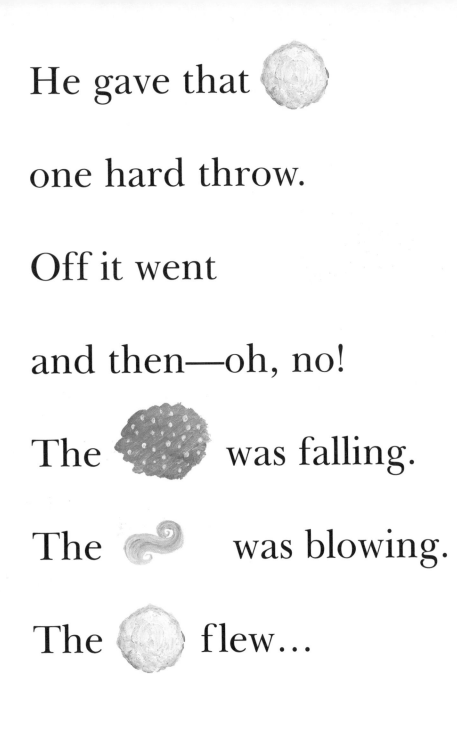 was blowing.

The 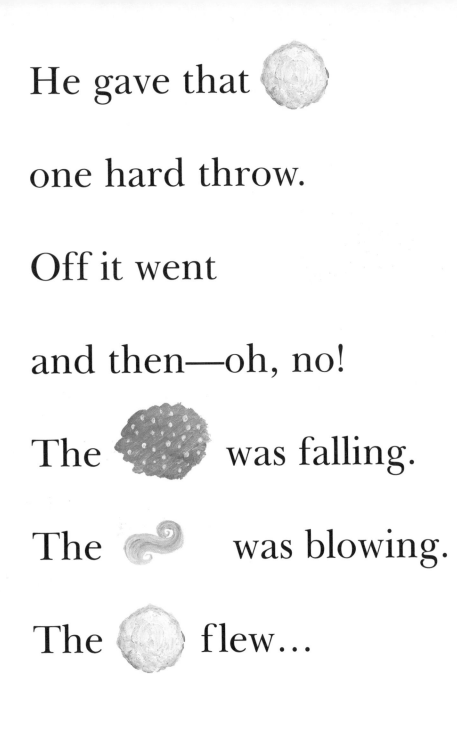 flew...

and kept on going!

It went past  and

on  .

It went over

everybody's .

It stopped the  .

It stopped the  .

It scared the

off some .

It chased away

a  and a  .

It knocked off

many people's  .

But still the

did not stop.

It flew into

the ice-cream shop.

And while Miss Jones

was on the ,

it dropped into

an ice-cream .

Just then, the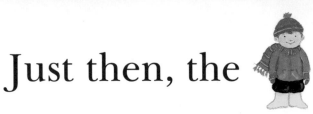

came in, of course.

He was as hungry

as a .

He wanted something

good to eat...

so with a

he bought a treat.

That's all.

No more !